SpongeBob LovePants

by Erica Pass
illustrated by Gregg Schigiel

Ready-to-Read

Simon Spotlight/Nickelodeon
New York   London   Toronto   Sydney

Based on the TV series *SpongeBob SquarePants*® created by Stephen Hillenburg as seen on Nickelodeon®

SIMON SPOTLIGHT
An imprint of Simon & Schuster Children's Publishing Division
1230 Avenue of the Americas, New York, New York 10020

6 8 10 9 7 5
Library of Congress Cataloging-in-Publication Data
Pass, Erica.
SpongeBob LovePants / by Erica Pass.- 1st ed.
p. cm. - (Ready-to-read)
"Based on the TV series SpongeBob SquarePants created by Stephen Hillenburg as seen on Nickelodeon."
ISBN-13: 978-1-4169-1758-8
ISBN-10: 1-4169-1758-6
I. Title: Sponge Bob LovePants. II. Title: SpongeBob Love Pants. III. SpongeBob SquarePants (Television program)
IV. Title. V. Series.
PZ7.P269367Sp 2007
[E]-dc22
2006003982

One morning SpongeBob
woke up in a very good mood.
Something felt different.

SpongeBob went to see
his friend Patrick.
"Can you smell it, Patrick?" he asked.
"The kelp is in bloom!
Love is in the air!"

Patrick sniffed.

"I don't smell anything," he said.

Just then Squidward came out
of his house to pick up the paper.
"Do you smell the love, Squidward?"
asked SpongeBob.

"No!" said Squidward.
He slammed his front door
as he went back inside.

"Gee, Squidward sure is grouchy today," SpongeBob said. "I wonder what will make him happy."
"Maybe he needs to smell the love," said Patrick.

"You're right, Patrick!" said SpongeBob.
"Maybe Squidward needs love in his life.
   Maybe we can help!"

SpongeBob and Patrick asked everyone
in Bikini Bottom if they wanted to
go on a date with Squidward.

"What a grouch," they said.

Just then Karla arrived.
She delivered fresh buns
to the Krusty Krab every day.
"Out of my way, Squid," she said.

"Oh, Karla," said Squidward.
"What a pleasure."
"Hmm," said SpongeBob.
"Maybe Karla would go out
    with Squidward."

SpongeBob came up with a plan.
"Karla, would you like to have
dinner with me tonight?" he asked.
"Why?" Karla replied.

"Love is in the air!"
 SpongeBob said.
"Well, all right," said Karla.
"I have no other plans."

After Karla left, SpongeBob
told Squidward, "I need you
to come to dinner tonight."
"No," said Squidward. "I am busy."
"No, you are not," said SpongeBob.
"Look at your calendar."

That evening SpongeBob and
Squidward went to the restaurant.
"What are you doing here?"
Karla asked Squidward.
"You tell me," said Squidward.

"Surprise!" said SpongeBob.
"I thought we could all
  enjoy a nice dinner together."
"I am not hungry," said Squidward.
"I have to go," said Karla.
"Please stay," said SpongeBob.

"Oh, fine," said Squidward.
"But not for long."
"That's for sure," said Karla.
SpongeBob clapped his hands.
"This will be great!" he said.

SpongeBob tried to get
Squidward and Karla to talk.
"Squidward plays the clarinet,"
SpongeBob said.

"I have heard," said Karla.
"It sounds squeaky."

"Aren't the buns that Karla
   delivers delicious?"
   asked SpongeBob.
"Not really," said Squidward,
"I think they are rather stale."

SpongeBob wanted the two
to get along.
But the only thing Squidward and
Karla had in common was that
they were both grumpy.

Finally SpongeBob had enough.
He began to cry.
"I cannot take this!" he said.
"I just wanted you both to be happy.
But all you ever do is fight!"

He blew his nose into his napkin
and ran off.

Squidward and Karla were quiet.
"I am glad he's gone,"
said Squidward.
"SpongeBob was only trying
to be kind," said Karla.

"Maybe if we were nice,
   he would feel better."
"Ah, then he would leave us alone!"
   said Squidward.

The next day at the Krusty Krab,
Karla arrived to deliver the buns.
"Good morning, Squidward!" she said.
"Beautiful day, isn't it?"

SpongeBob smiled.
Maybe Squidward and Karla
would fall in love after all!
"Love is in the air!" he said
as he swept the floor.

As soon as SpongeBob walked away,
Squidward told Karla,
"The only thing in the air I smell
is stale patty buns."
"Did you forget about the sound
of your rotten clarinet playing?"
Karla asked.

The two of them laughed.
"You know, maybe we do get along,"
Squidward said.

Just then SpongeBob came over.

"Ah, the smell of love is so sweet," SpongeBob said.

Squidward and Karla rolled their eyes.

"Here we go again!" they said.